CLAUDIA BOLDT

YOU'RE A RUDE PIG, BERTIE!

To Simon, Luis, and Kio

First published by Random House Children's Publishers, UK, 2013.
Copyright © Claudia Boldt 2013.
First published in the United States in 2013, by NorthSouth Books Inc.,
an imprint of NordSüd Verlag AG, CH-8005 Zürich, Switzerland.

The right of Claudia Boldt to be identified as the author of this work has been
asserted in accordance with the Copyright, Designs and Patents Act 1988.

Distributed in the United States by NorthSouth Books Inc., New York 10016.
Library of Congress Cataloging-in-Publication Data is available.
ISBN: 978-0-7358-4152-9 (trade edition)
Printed in China by Toppan Leefung Packaging & Printing (Dongguan) Co., Ltd.,
Dongguan, P.R.C., May 2013
1 3 5 7 9 · 10 8 6 4 2
www.northsouth.com

CLAUDIA BOLDT

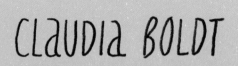

YOU'RE A RUDE PIG,
BERTiE!

**North
South**

Bertie was a most unpleasant pig. He thought of no one but himself.

Every morning he looked in the mirror and said, "Who is the most beautiful piglet in the world? It is me, myself, and I—wonderful Monsieur Pig — Bertie the Pig!"

Bertie always had something nasty to say about everyone he met.

"Dreadful hair today, Mrs. Harley!"

"Without your annoying husband, Mrs. Block?"

"Long time no see, Mrs. Breun.
You look older!"

"Joseph! Your bad smell never ceases to amaze me!"

It was no wonder that Bertie had no friends.

But one day Bertie met Ruby. She was the cutest
rabbit he had ever seen, and to Bertie's surprise
he found himself saying, "Your ears are so long.
How extraordinarily beautiful!"

Ruby was very flattered and gave him
an extra big piece of cheese.

Chèvr
Feta
Edam
Gouda
Leerdammer
Shropshire Blue
Muenster cheese

ch se
Ch ay
Hal mi
Dam lue
chee
E p
Bonifa

On the way home, Bertie bumped into Roland the sausage dog, who could not believe his ears when Bertie said, "What a lovely day! And look at you; you are looking splendid!"

All day he could think of nothing but Ruby and how nice she was. Bertie decided to impress her by throwing a huge party.

He wrote special invitations
to everyone.

If she came he would even show her
his big collection of marble eggs.
Nothing seemed to be too great an effort.

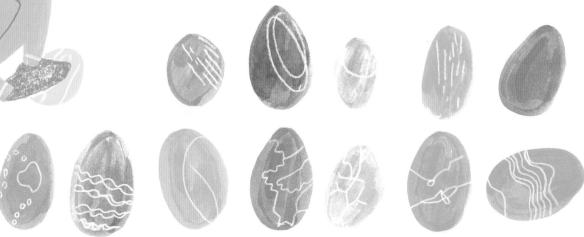

Bertie's invitations were sent out, and the party was the talk of the town. But Ruby was not impressed that Bertie had insulted all of her friends. In fact everyone had had enough of him and his rudeness.

THESE ARE JUST a FEW OF THE DISHES BERTIE PREPARED.

It was the day of the party, and at three o'clock everything was ready. But no one came. Bertie was disappointed. "Where is everyone? Didn't they receive their invitations? Doesn't Ruby like me?"

Bertie went to bed early after his miserable day.

Bertie woke up all sweaty and upset. "The toothbrush is right! This is terrible. . . . Is this why no one has come to my party?"

Bertie wanted to get some fresh air to forget about his nightmare, so he went for a walk.

There was Hildegard. "Hey, Hildegard! I . . ." But she had already turned her back on him.

Then he saw Mrs. Harley and said, "Hello!" But she did not even grace him with a look in return.

Then Bertie heard Arnold whispering, "That pig is so rude. He will never have any friends."

Bertie was very sad and decided that some cheese would cheer him up. He got in line next to Mr. Wolf.

Mr. Wolf was annoyed that he had to wait and grumbled:
"Hurry up! Can't you hear me? What are those silly long
ears good for anyway? If . . ."

He could not finish his sentence because Bertie
grunted very loudly, "Don't speak to Ruby like that!"

"That was nice, Bertie," said Ruby.
Bertie blushed and said,
"Really?! Thank you!"

People smiled at Bertie,
and Arnold even nodded
his approval.

Finally Bertie knew what to do. . . .

This time everyone came, apart from
Mrs. Harley, who still held a grudge.
But most important of all, Ruby was there,
and it was the best party ever!